I0649108

Eva Katherine Clapp

A Woman's Triumph

A True Story of Western Life

Eva Katherine Clapp

A Woman's Triumph
A True Story of Western Life

ISBN/EAN: 9783742811332

Manufactured in Europe, USA, Canada, Australia, Japa

Cover: Foto ©Andreas Hilbeck / pixelio.de

Manufactured and distributed by brebook publishing software
(www.brebook.com)

Eva Katherine Clapp

A Woman's Triumph

A
WOMAN'S TRIUMPH

A TRUE STORY

OF

WESTERN LIFE

CHICAGO
A. H. Andrews & Co
1885

A Woman's Triumph.

"Pure, with all faithful passion—fair—
    With tender smiles, that come and go,
And comforting as April air
    After the snow."

"THEY will try very hard to win you away from me, dearest."

"That they can never do."

"It is true that I am not worthy of you. Where is the man who is? Hannah, be patient with my failings; you know them well. My life is in your hands; you alone can redeem me, for I love you with all my heart. See what a slight, blue-veined

wrist you have, child; I could break it like
a reed. Yet you are the stronger of the
two. Are you not afraid? Think well
before you answer. I am in deadly earnest, and once you are really mine, I will
never give you up."

"I am not afraid—not in the least
afraid, Dick."

"You will need all your quiet strength
of character, Hannah."

"*Love* is strong and must prevail."

"I believe people are jealous when they
see a bit of honest happiness, there is so
little of it to be found."

"*We* will triumph over them, Dick."

"I trust so, but my heart misgives me. We shall see."

All around them are smiling fields, covered with sheaves of yellow wheat, and the gray old farm-house beyond seems to doze and dream in the sleepy afternoon.

Hannah was just eighteen the summer Dick came to work for her father on the big McClean farm, celebrated all over the country for its fifteen hundred acres of fertile land, as well as for its owner's eccentric ways, and his two pretty daughters. A close man was old John McClean, of Scotch descent. He had made his money by hard work and was jealous lest a gay son-in-law should some day after his death squander any part of the estate he had accumulated and of which he was so proud.

His second wife, Hannah's step-mother, knew well how to play upon the old man's pet theories, and her own daughter Ruth had been well educated, while Hannah had left the district school at fifteen to assist in the housework. Yet as she was passionately fond of reading, her mind was better stored with general knowledge than Ruth's. The latter, however, had learned to play a few waltzes and polkas upon the piano, which went far to convince her father that Ruth was quite a musical genius, and that

the money spent upon her had been well
invested. Ruth was a blonde with a wealth
of bright hair and cheeks like a ripe peach.
She was also rather lazy and selfish. These
faults were, however, not to be wondered
at, since her mother humored her every
whim.

When Dick Barry came, Ruth looked
upon him with a mixture of scorn and
admiration—scorn for his poverty and
position, admiration for his fine figure, his
easy bearing, and sunny, pleasant ways.
For say what we may, while it takes more
than one generation to give that noble,
nameless grace which denotes the born

gentleman, it also takes more than one generation of drinking and thriftlessness to efface the stamp of good breeding.

Though Dick, owing to his father's neglect, was ignorant of books, and poor as a church mouse, still the Barrys had once been a family noted for refinement and culture. The sayings of the old judge, Dick's grandfather, were yet quoted in many a court of law.

Hannah was at first extremely shy and reserved in her manner toward him, persistently ignoring the half sad, and yet proud, glance of entreaty he was wont unconsciously to cast toward her. At their country parties and sociables, while she laughed and chatted with a more prosperous rival, he sat aloof. Yet she could not but divine the reason why he always disappeared when Frank Dennison came over with his bay horses summer evenings to ask her to drive, and it pained her to see him come in late, looking pale and haggard. They said he had inherited his father's fatal appetite for liquor, but Hannah certainly never saw him in the least under its influence. To her he was always reserved, though watchful of her least wish, and ready with his life, if need be, to serve her. She was his goddess, whom he " worshiped

in secret, and from afar." His mother died
when he was born, and Hannah was the
only good and gracious woman he had ever
known.

One day as Ruth was making some half
jesting, yet wholly tantalizing and imper-
tinent remark about Dick's quiet homage
of Hannah, her father, taking his usual
noonday rest in the vine-covered porch,
heard the girl's idle talk through the open
window. Coming in soon after, the grim
old farmer turned to his elder daughter
more sternly than the occasion seemed to
warrant.

"Hannah,if you are encouraging Richard

Barry, you are preparing for him a bitter disappointment. I am sorry a girl of mine should be so light and wicked as to enjoy making a fool of any man. Dick has his fine traits, but you know I would rather see you buried than married to a drinking man. Don't talk to me about reform—it's no use. If a man cannot respect himself enough to keep straight when he is single he'll never improve when he marries—rather go down hill all the time, and drag you with him—mark my words for it."

So saying the old man strode away, while Ruth laughed and ran lightly to her room to take a nap before dressing for the afternoon.

Hannah went quietly to her favorite retreat, wearied, troubled, saddened almost beyond endurance. An hour or two later, it must have been fate that brought Dick up from the hay-field through the orchard path to the house, instead of round by the usual road. Hannah had thrown herself down on the grass under the big tree in the orchard corner, and was weeping. Dick, hurrying along, water-jug in hand, nearly stumbled over the disconsolate little heap of pink calico.

"Oh! please pardon me," he said softly,

pausing, " I did not see you." Hannah
flushed scarlet, the blood crimsoning her
throat and ears which alone were visible.
Then, as she bashfully lifted her face and
made an effort to rise, he saw that she had
been crying. Then the big, reckless fellow,
who was afraid of nothing human, trembled
as he stood, pale and stammering, before the
girl he loved madly and hopelessly. "What
is the matter? who has been treating you
badly? Tell me, Hannah," he asked after
a moment's pause, as she again buried her
face in her hands. He tenderly took both
of those sun-burned, toil-worn, useful little
hands in his own. "*Please* don't cry,

Hannah, it makes me feel so to see you unhappy. Don't, I cannot bear it, because I cannot comfort you, and I love you so dearly. How can I help it since I know what you are, and see you every day. I ought not to have come here."

She did not reply, and he continued bitterly: "I know I am a worthless fellow, not fit for a girl like you. I have been fool enough to think at times that I could put by all my wasted past, and with a little hope in my heart go away to labor and win a fortune for you, so proving to your father that I am a man. But Frank Dennison could place you at once where you belong,

in a pleasant home of your own. He is
well off, and I—I have not a cent. I see
he is over again to-day. His bays are
hitched at the gate. You had better go
in, Hannah, it's not Ruth he comes to see."

"He can wait," she answered quietly.
Something in her tear-stained, wistful face
made Dick's heart beat with a sudden, pas-
sionate hope. He drew her toward him.
"Oh Hannah, my darling, if I could only
win you for a wife, I would prove to your
father how steady and sober I can be. Could
you ever learn to care for me a little?"

"You must not ask me, Dick. Be sober
and good for your *own* sake, because it is

right to be so, because it is a sin and shame for a young man like you to waste your life.   Think what a man your grandfather, Judge Barry, was!"

" Yes, but he had an education," said Dick sorrowfully.

" True, but think how many uneducated, poor men have risen to be great and successful by their own brave and patient efforts."

Their conversation was interrupted by Ruth, who came tripping airily toward them, in fresh muslins, to inform her crumpled and tearful sister of Mr. Dennison's arrival.   " And if you don't look out,

Hannah," she added saucily, "I'll get him away from you—see if I don't—if I *am* only sixteen and a half."

And so poor Dick was answered. All that afternoon he worked in the hot hay-field with a wild energy that tasked the other men sorely. The hot sun blazed down upon the meadows, and, like one in a dream, he heard all day the rattle of the mower and the shouts to the horses as they lagged in their walk.

Frank Dennison in the cool parlor did not find the heat uncomfortable; neither did the blonde and languid Ruth who entertained him, looking like a blue-bell in her

azure muslin robes. She played and sang
for him, but Hannah withdrew to the
kitchen early, saying, "The men will need
a tempting supper after such a hot day in
the field." Then she baked divers dainty
things, and finally brewed a pitcherful of
some cooling drink, and donning a wide
shade-hat, carried it out to the workers.
Mrs. McClean was taking an afternoon
nap. On this dreamy, drowsy day the old
farm-house was very quiet. A lazy bee
droned idly above the blossoms in the
garden. The white kitten played with a
spool of thread. Ruth, in a low. soft
voice, read aloud a verse or two from a

volume of poems she was showing Dennison. Suddenly, into the midst of all this
sweet peace, came Hannah, breathless,
pale. "Ruth," she said, in a strange, hushed
voice, "father has had a sunstroke, and
they are bringing him to the house. We
must send for the doctor. Let us get the
room ready."

"Oh! Hannah, is he dead? Do not let
me see him," cried Ruth, beginning to weep
nervously.

"Hush, hush," said the elder sister
sternly.

"I will go for Doctor Meade," said
Dennison, and just then Dick and

Norwegian Pete came in bringing the old
farmer unconscious between them. He
was breathing heavily.

Hannah, who loved her father faithfully,
in spite of his gruff, ungracious speeches
to her, felt her heart sink with fear as she
watched him lying there.

When the doctor came he gave him a
few drops of stimulating mixture, and put
crushed ice upon his head. He revived
somewhat, and by the following day had
so far recovered as to begin worrying about
his hay crop.

"It will be ruined now," he said dole-
fully, "for this fine weather cannot last

much longer. If we only had some one
to drive the mower, we might get that
meadow finished in a day or two; but it's
just the busy time."

Hannah, seeing it troubled her father
greatly, at last suggested driving the mower
herself until other help could be procured.
At first farmer McClean pooh poohed at
this idea, only to yield later. And so the
young girl went out the next day to drive
in the big meadow, while Mrs. McClean
stayed by her husband's bedside, and pretty,
idle Ruth grumbled much as she ruefully
undertook the work of kitchen and dairy.

The saying that "misfortunes never

come singly " was verified that week at
the homestead, for that day, about eleven
o'clock, as everything was going on peace-
fully and regularly in the field, and Farmer
McClean was dozing, soothed to sleep by
what was music to his ears, the clatter of
the mowing machine, what should the
horses do but run into a nest of wild
bumble bees, of which the meadow happened to be full. Of course the insects
attacked the horses fiercely, and when the
maddened creatures ran, Pete's cries of
" Whoa, Whoa!" only frightened them
the more. Then it was that Dick jumped
down from the stack he was rounding

off, cleared the distance between himself and the horses with a few bounds, and seized them by the bits. He was just in time, for Hannah could not have clung to her high seat much longer, and the sharp sickle would no doubt have cut her fearfully.

Dick was the only one hurt. In the excitement he said nothing about his wrist, which was badly cut.

As he was walking to the house with Hannah, she noticed his left hand wrapped in a handkerchief and partly thrust beneath the breast of his working blouse.

"You are hurt," she said compassionately.

"Only a scratch," was the reply, though his pallor betrayed loss of blood and pain.

Arrived at the house they met Dennison, who had driven over with the doctor. It was found that a small artery had been severed in Dick's effort to lift Hannah from her seat upon the mower.

The old farmer fretted and fumed at this fresh accident, and the delay it would occasion in the work. No one seemed to realize how perilous Hannah's position had been—how narrow her escape from death. Dick realized it, however, as he leaned against a pillar of the veranda after

having his hand bound up. He was gloom-
ily watching the dark clouds in the western
sky, as Hannah, pale, tearful, yet with a
sweeter smile for him than he had ever
seen upon her face before, came out and
thanked him earnestly. Soon after, when
tea was ready, he declined joining the
others, but insisted upon going out to help
Pete cap the unfinished stack, before the
rain should reach it.

"How could you be so careless, Hannah,
as to drive into the midst of those bees?
Didn't you know they were there? Of
course the horses ran." This consoling
remark proceeded from Mrs. McClean as

she was pouring out tea.

"Oh! she was too busy watching Dick at work to have all her thoughts about her. Now, Hannah, since Dick came to grief through you, seems to me you ought to go out and help him finish that stack," chimed in Ruth satirically.

All was still, the heat was oppressive, and in dread of the coming thunderstorm the fowls had sought the shelter of the house wall, and hovered near, clucking to each other in a sagacious way, as weatherwise old people discuss the prospects of a storm.

Out upon the shadowy vine-covered porch no one heard a step or divined that the man they were so carelessly discussing had just come up from work and was resting there for a moment.

Dennison laughed slightly at Ruth's speech, then bowing to Hannah as if in apology for this, added: "Far more likely that Dick came to grief through his old failing. Poor whisky imbibed too freely under a hot sun does not tend to make a man clear-headed."

Hannah's voice, pure and silver-toned as a bell, and bearing in it a pointed rebuke, came through the window to Dick.

"You are mistaken, all of you. You do not seem to understand that Dick had nothing whatever to do with the horses when they started, and as for his drinking, I know he has not touched a drop of intoxicating drink for weeks. His courage saved my life, for I could not have kept my seat one moment longer."

"I am sure, Miss Hannah, that any man might be willing to risk more than he has to-day, to find so earnest a champion," said Doctor Meade.

"I hate *injustice,* that is all," was her reply.

"Dick is not so bad a fellow," said Dennison patronizingly. "He has been remarkably steady this summer, but he will

never make a success in life. He will work
far better for others than he will for himself."

Hannah's voice as she answered was
slightly tremulous.

" Do you know, Mr. Dennison, I am
often tempted to rebel against the narrow-
ness of the definition which most people
give to that term—'success in life.' Now
to succeed in getting money is no doubt a
fine thing, and not so exceedingly difficult
either, when one has been left a fair capital,
as you have."

" It requires as much business ability to
keep money as it does to make it," said

Mrs. McClean sagely. The latter was one of those who generally save themselves the trouble and responsibility of original opinion, by a proverb or popular aphorism, cut, dried, and ready to apply to all cases.

"Saving money comes so naturally to many people that it is changed from an admirable quality to a passion," said Hannah drily. The latent sarcasm in her voice made Dennison flush slightly as she continued. "And then I so much dislike to hear people talk as though temperance, undoubtedly a great virtue, was the *only* one. Is it nothing to be brave, generous, charitable?"

" You are nervous, Hannah," said her step-mother; " surely it would be well for you to get a breath of air out on the porch."

The girl arose, all the blood in her tired frame throbbing indignantly.

There was a rustle among the vines; Dick was just going down the steps. From the pallor of his fine face his eyes shone with excitement and wounded pride.

Hannah rushed past him on her way to the orchard. She felt that she must be alone, but the young man followed her, and as she sank down upon her favorite seat he laid his hand upon her dark hair reverently.

" Hannah," he began, pain giving his words earnestness and dignity, " I may not have another opportunity to speak to you for I am going away to-night, and must thank you for standing up for me so bravely. I did not intend to listen, but was on the porch and heard all they said. You were right—I had not been drinking to-day. Indeed I never touch liquor now, but—there it is, my bad name clings to me."

" Where are you going?" she asked.

" Up north, to the lumber regions. A man can get good wages in the pineries, they say. God bless you, I shall love you

always and be a better man for having
known you."

" Dick," she urged, " such a rough, hard
life as you will have to lead there, and
right in the midst of temptation!"

"Oh! well, who cares?" he said sadly.

" I care," said Hannah," her true woman-
hood speaking in her voice.

"Hannah! Do you care enough to
promise me that you will some day become
my wife?" he said. "Not now, I am poor
and struggling. I would not ask you to
share my lot."

"Do you think, then, that I could bear
to live on here, in peace and with plenty,

and let you brave danger and hardship all alone? No, no, I will be to you a helper, a blessing, Richard, or nothing! We will share life together, both in trouble and in joy."

He held her to his breast one moment, and as he realized how great a gift was this noble wonan's love, felt that a lifetime of devotion alone could repay her generous faith.

Of course there was bitter opposition from her father when Hannah told him of her promise; and a few months later, when they were married, he refused to be present, and she went away without his farewell or blessing. This did not make the new life of toil and privation any easier. But Hannah never murmured. She had the spirit and patience of an old Scotch covenanter when she believed she was in the right.

When Hannah's little son was born she named him John, after her father, and sent the baby's picture to him with an affectionate letter.

But the old farmer was lying in his coffin when it arrived.

Later, when his will was read, it was found he had given nearly everything to Ruth, after providing for his wife.

Hannah's portion was to be given to her only on condition that she should leave her husband and come back to live on the old farm.

Frank Dennison was appointed administrator of the estate.

When Hannah read the cold, formal letter in which Lawyer Keene informed her of this, she could scarcely realize the extent of the injustice toward her.

*   *   *   *   *   *   *   *

A pale northern sky, gloomy forests on either hand, and on the banks of a broad, rushing river a cluster of log-houses— these make up the picture.

It is spring-time, and the air is fragrant with woodland odors.

A great colony of water fowl have just passed over the hamlet. They flew in a straight line, in orderly time-honored fashion, well marshaled by their captain. They were glad to breathe again the resinous-scented air of their northern pine woods, for they had traveled hundreds of miles from Florida's groves of orange trees and low-lying reedy marshes by the warm, blue sea. They were so near their summer home, as they flew over Mishawamee, that they began to congratulate themselves upon their safe arrival.

Hannah put down for a moment the heavy pail of water she was carrying to the house, and looked up to watch their graceful flight, and listen to their shrill voice. Then she said with a little sigh, "Yes, the wild geese are back again. Spring will soon be here now, and I am glad enough, it has been such a long, hard winter."

Thus musing she passed into the little cottage that was their home.

From the scattered houses blue smoke rose in the clear, still air. The forest, vast, dark and mysterious stretched its huge arms around the settlement, and the cold

sky of the north, with its oppressive melancholy, like a haunting, monotonous song
whose minor tones suggest loss and desola-
tion, brooded over all.

Soon the big logs would come floating
down the swift current of Wolf River,
and the wild songs of the adventurous
raftsmen would waken the echoes in those
sleeping forest aisles. A dare-devil set
were these lumbermen of the north. A
reckless, red-shirted, picturesque band of
crusaders, whose arms were turned against
the sturdy trees. With much of the law-
lessness and ignorance, though very little
of the piety, of those mail-clad hordes of

the middle ages, who went out to fight
the Moslem, these men fought against
unrelenting enemies too—against the bitter
cold of the long winters, when feet and
hands were frozen by exposure to the cruel
air; against the home-sickness and despondency natural to a lot so isolated, so full
of hardship and of danger. What wonder
that they drank, sometimes until look or
word provoked the fierce quarrel, which
ended, perhaps, in bloodshed, or in crime!

Yet most of the dwellers in Mishawamee
were contented enough. It was as cheerful and refined a life as any they had ever
known. But it was not so with Hannah.

The three years she had spent there seemed an eternity. She was of finer mold than the heavy Norwegian or Swedish wives who largely composed the female portion of the settlement. She could not speak to them of sorrow or aspirations that to them were wholly incomprehensible. So her heart was full of a great hunger for some slight measure of sympathy, of confidence from one of her own sex. Day by day her great patient, black eyes carried the pathetic shadow of her longing in their depths, and her well-cut, refined features grew more sharp, her cheek thinner.

She was a slender, nervous, ambitious

little American woman. The privations she had borne, the struggles against poverty and despondency had never even been hinted at by her to any of her former friends, and she was far too proud and independent to admit to those who blamed or pitied her for her choice, that her life with Dick Barry so far had been a constant struggle to keep up *his* courage as well as her own.

Poor Dick, though always kind and brave, did indeed seem to be dogged by some malicious spirit of ill-luck. Hannah had not undergone quite such marvelous misfortunes, it is true, as that mariner in

"Billee Taylor" who was "bitten by a crocodile" and "swallowed by a whale, all on account of Eliza," but she had been scorched by throes of fever brought on by overwork and exposure to cold, to say nothing of mental troubles, care and sorrow, all on account of Dick.

But if you imagine for a moment that she wavered, or loved him less, you know little of a true woman's heart. Undoubtedly, Hannah was illogical enough to cling all the more tenderly to him with each misfortune. Her old-fashioned, unenlightened mind argued that when the world battered the poor fellow most heartlessly,

then he had most need of the devotion of
his wife, and the best right to it.

Only a farmer's daughter, and brought
up in the agricultural districts, she knew
little of that selfish philosophy which
would have advised her to take the child
and leave Dick to his fate, thus causing
herself to be included in the prosperous
majority. Hannah had always from a child
mended the broken legs of forlorn birds,
and nursed the weak lambkins back to life
and vigor; usually to have the latter taken
from her and sold as soon as they grew
frolicsome and had attained good condition under her sheltering care.

It had been a trying winter for the little family, for Dick the husband and father had been ill for nearly a month during the coldest weather, and as their home was mortgaged, it had taxed Hannah's strength to the utmost to provide the few comforts he required, and save a small sum toward the first payment of the mortgage, which came due in spring. But she was a brave little woman, and worked on faithfully, taking in washing or sewing for the mill hands and lumbermen, so that by the first of April she had saved nearly enough money to make the first payment on the home.

Seventy-five dollars was all she had put by thus far, and the sum required was one hundred and ten.

The very pain it caused him to see his wife and child suffer made Dick rush away from the place, but Hannah did not think of this, and those winter days when he buttoned up his shabby overcoat sadly and went out into the storm, she put aside her work, took the child in her arms, and wept over him.

The weather was bitterly cold, and the little family suffered at times for want of proper food and warmer clothing. But April came and with it warmer days.

Hannah began to take heart again. Finally she received a letter one day when Dick was out in the woods. It was from Mr. Dennison, advising her to leave her husband and come home. He had heard how hard she worked, how poor she was (the letter said), and it grieved him.

Hannah put the letter away in her work-box. She was angry at its patronizing tone, and, womanlike, wished to spare Dick the unpleasant feelings which the reading of it would occasion his proud nature. She intended to treat it with quiet contempt, and to speak of it to no one.

As she looked about her poor little room,

how scantily furnished and bare it looked!
In one corner stood a bed covered with gay
patchwork,—a quilt that Hannah's own
mother in years gone by had pieced for her
baby daughter, no doubt dreaming fondly
as mothers will, of the pretty child's future,
and little guessing that Hannah would ever
gaze upon it with wistful eyes in this
bleak northern hamlet. The floor was
bare, though white with much scrubbing.
A small calico curtain hung at each of the
two small windows, and partly obscured a
view of snowy wastes, pine woods half
buried in big drifts, and a few rude shan-
ties. The only bright objects about the

place were the wreath of autumn leaves around the wedding certificate that hung upon the wall, and baby Jack's rosy cheeks as he slept softly in his cradle.

"So they want me to leave Dick! leave my husband! *Never*—not for all the farms in Illinois!" said Hannah aloud. Then as she looked at the little sleeper and realized the wrong this was to him, and thought of the education and chance in life a little of this money would have enabled her to give her child, big tears rolled down her patient face. A few moments of inner conflict and her rare spirit reasserted itself, a flush of defiance came to that thin cheek which a few years before had been softly rounded, richly tinted as the peach.

"Never mind, my bonny lad," she whispered softly, stooping over the cradle and kissing the boy's forehead, "we will never ask them for a cent. Let us all perish together, if need be, rather than submit to cruel, wicked conditions like these."

Yet it did seem hard and cruel, for she had been a faithful, hard-working girl at home, and her own mother had brought a fair dowry when she married, all of which had gone into the farm and its improvements.

Hannah wrote a letter home telling them to keep the money, and never write to her again.

The next winter was a severe one. Dick was laid up for weeks with pneumonia, and as he could earn nothing, Hannah washed for the men at the saw-mill, until finally her wrists became so lame and swollen that the pain scarcely allowed her any sleep. Yet no word of complaint found its way to the old farmhouse. She felt her relatives were dead to her, and would have worked with bleeding feet and hands rather than ask aid from them.

Of late she could not conceal from her-

self the sad fact that Dick, for whose sake
she had lost her heritage, was not the man
she had hoped her courageous example
would have made him.   As soon as he was
able to walk again, he seemed eager to get
away from her presence—not to find work
that he might lift the too heavy burden
from her patient shoulders, but rather to
seek in Joe Murphy's saloon the stimulus
that enabled him to forget for awhile all
care and misery.

Yet Hannah said little, but worked on,
and felt keenly the change in him. Little
Jack often patted her cheek, saying softly,
" Mamma looks sorry."

Poor Dick! it was not that he meant to be cruel. Capable of rising at times to grand heights of courage and endeavor, he possessed no power of patient endurance. It had hurt his pride cruelly, too, her father thus taking it for granted that unless it was secured by this condition Hannah's portion would be squandered by her husband. Although he had borne the cold without complaint, he was not well, and indeed had always possessed less physical strength than nerve and spirit, which caused him to dash at a hard task and accomplish it by sheer pluck, as a gallant French soldier might charge recklessly at

the enemy.   But this method of work
told but poorly in the pineries, against the
stolid force of his companions.   And then
a jealous pain always tugged at his heart
as he watched his wife's sad face.   He
thought she might regret her impulsive
answer when he had asked her to marry
him, and that now, when he stood in the
way of her obtaining her fortune, she pos-
sibly might feel relieved to be free from
him, good though he was, and loyal and
tender as ever.   It was scarcely a comfortable home that he could now make for her
and the boy.

With other wants, Hannah's faded

cotton gown, he thought, was not sufficient-
ly warm. The man's heart grew bitter,
defiant against fate as he watched her at
work one dreary March day. A biting
wind was sweeping round the walls of the
little cottage, driving in snow at every
nook and cranny. The loosened windows
rattled in the blast. The sky was dark
and lowering. Evidently a blizzard was
brewing in the upper lake region.
Hannah, with a pale face, was preparing
to place the wash-boiler upon the stove,
where green wood sputtered and smoked,
giving out more steam and sap than heat.
Their supply of dry wood had been

exhausted during Dick's illness. The baby played quietly on the floor, but his little shoes were worn out at the toes.

" The child needs new shoes," said Dick, listlessly.   " I wish I could get my strength back again."

" Yes," replied Hannah, " I don't like to spend a cent of the money I have saved for paying off the mortgage."

The man made no reply.   He looked vacantly before him, as if fixing his thoughts upon some atom in the thin air. He then rose slowly, and with an evident effort to control his emotion, walked from the cottage.

Hannah resumed her work.

That evening when he returned home, she left him with the child, while she stepped into a neighbor's on an arrand. Dick went to the work-box to find a pencil to cast up his accounts with his employer, as he had now been at work for several days. Seeing Dennison's letter lying there, he, of course, read it, and wondered why Hannah had not told him of it before. He was indignant at its tone. But the chief pain came from a suspicion that his wife had been influenced by it, and intended to act upon its advice, else why should she have kept it from him? He

knew all her loyalty, her goodness, but his
lack of faith was in himself, in his power
to keep her love, since he had failed to
make the happy, comfortable home for her
that he had intended to when they were
married.   Yet he was fully conscious that
buried away beneath a mass of faults and
weaknesses there was a manliness, yes, a
power of self-sacrifice for those he loved
that Dennison, prosperous and pompous,
was utterly incapable of even compre-
hending.

This was a new blow, and just as he had
begun to take fresh heart from the spring
weather and was maturing a plan which

bid fair to succeed—a plan that would en-
able him to take Hannah away, and place
her in a pretty cottage amid the flowers
and trees of a more genial climate. He
meant to surprise her with this. It de-
pended upon the answer his employer, a
capitalist and owner of a ranch in California, would give him within the next three
days; and now, perhaps, she was coldly
thinking of leaving him!

She came in looking quite cheerful, and
smiling kindly. He had folded the letter,
placing it carefully back in the box,
and sat with bowed head, scarcely looking up as she came in. Hannah rocked

little Jack to sleep, looking wistfully at her husband.

"You are ill. I am afraid you are working too hard before your strength has returned. That attack of pneumonia has left you weak," she said.

He made no reply. Then hoping to beguile him from his sorrowful mood, she continued cheerfully, "I am so glad spring has come. As soon as we can find time let us have the garden ploughed. I mean to have a fine garden this summer."

"I don't think we can make any plans, Hannah, for the future. You were foolish to marry me, and I was wicked to ask you, but I loved you. Ah! well, better leave me to my fate, take the boy and go home."

He said this more in hope of hearing her denial of any such thought than really meaning it. But her loyal, suffering heart was stung to be thus doubted, or it was possible she thought that he was really tired of her. Oh, that was a cruel, maddening thought! She loved him, yet he must not think she would weakly cling to a man who did not care for her, who would not also cleave to her through every storm and trouble. She clasped Jack's little sleeping form to her heart, and paused a moment before replying. She did not choose that he should find her voice trembling.

"Very well, but I supposed you had more independence and pride than to allow your wife to go back to those who would insult *you.*"

Dick, whose head seemed to be on fire and his heart like ice at this, their first quarrel, rose abruptly and left the house. It was late when he returned and the subject was not renewed.

Hannah found he had prepared his own breakfast and gone away much earlier than usual the next morning.

It was late when she awoke from a

troubled sleep. All that day she went over in her mind their brief married life. Poor Dick had worked very hard, but they had labored under great disadvantages, beginning life with almost nothing. Then she remembered how he looked that day when the horses ran away with the mower, and he had saved her life. She feared she had been wrong in not frankly showing Dennison's letter to him, then tearing it to pieces before him, and reassuring him of her devotion, of her scorn of any proposal to leave him. Thus she reproached herself, full of tender contrition.

It was late that afternoon when her

work was over. The room in order, she
dressed herself in a dark merino that Dick
had always liked to see her in. It was her
one good dress, and her eyes sparkled with
quite the old-time lustre as she thought
how kind she would be to Dick when he
came in. After all, love was enough, she
thought, and if they but worked on together with hope and courage fortune
could not fail to come some day.

" Papa will be here soon, now," she said
gayly to Jack, taking him in her arms to
the door, and looking up the long stretch
of road toward the woods and the planing-
mill.

A man was running toward the house. It was Neal Peterson, one of the workmen, not Dick. He came up breathlessly.

"Oh, Mrs. Barry, they sent me to tell you!" He paused. A rough, kindly Norwegian, he dreaded to tell this unsuspecting woman his sad message.

She waited, all the blood ebbing back to her heart.

"Your husband, Mrs. Barry—he went down into the new well they are digging—it caved in—"

"Is he dead?" she half whispered.

"We cannot tell—the men are digging —it was very deep."

" Then there is yet hope," she said.   At once she hastened on with Neal, the baby in her arms.   The men were still digging where the well had crumbled in, the perspiration standing out upon each forehead as they labored.

"Can he live or breathe under all that earth?" she asked, with pallid lips, of a man standing near.   He did not answer her, but turned away at the sight of her agonized face, muttering an evasion.   She remained there watching them, looking like a statue of despair, unconscious of anything but the utter horror of the calamity.

The sun went down. From the great woods came the melancholy hoot of an owl. The workmen paused. There was a brief consultation. Then one of them came to her.

" Have you found him?" she whispered. " Have you found his poor, dead body? Oh, let me go to him!"

" No, ma'am, its not that," said the man, " but they do say as how the well was almost two hundred feet dug out already, and there ain't a shadow of hope for him bein' alive, and ye see, ma'am, as it's Saturday night, we thought we would rest and then dig again Monday mornin'."

Hannah was roused at last from her stupor.

"Yet it may be that his breath still lingers." The thought came quickly to her mind.

" No, I beg you to go on—I will return to the house—I have a little money that I have saved—you can divide it among you, but do not leave the work."

She then went back to the house, took the little hoard saved for the mortgage, and carried it out to the men. They were idle, sitting in groups.

" Ma'am, you need the money for your child and yourself."

"Never mind, only commence your work again," and they began again to work vigorously. Half an hour passed in silence. Again they lagged.

"It is no use, ma'am, he is buried already, dead hours ago; it caves in almost as fast as we work, the soil is so loose here."

Hannah seized a spade. "Let me work with you," she cried. "Something tells me that my husband lives. Take every cent of the money, and when it is gone you can stop, but I will work on!"

Then, as though in reply to her, a faint, faint sound, as of a strong man's last cry for help, comes from beneath the mass of

crumbling earth at her feet! He has heard
her brave words. He lives.

Poor Dick had just started to come up
when the well began to give way, but a
ladder that he had taken down with him
leaned slantingly against the wall, and
kept much of the earth off, as he crouched
in the hollow thus formed. The foul air
had caused him to fall into a state of un-
consciousness, from which his wife's voice
had roused him, for he had heard her last
speech to the men, and had just enough
strength remaining to cry out with all his
fast failing power. In his suspense as to
whether they would abandon the work or

not, he gnawed a leather belt that he wore into pieces. (Hannah keeps the metal clasps of that belt among her treasured relics to this day.)

When a few moments later they carried him up and out into the air, they saw by the light of their lanterns that his hair had turned quite white.

He lay quietly upon his own bed a few hours later. The curious neighbors had departed.

The early sun peeped in at the window and kissed the face of baby Jack in his cradle, softly sleeping. It formed a halo around Hannah's head, as she leaned over Richard, bathing his temples with camphor. He was still very faint and ill but his heart was full of peace and humble thankfulness. He feebly tried to kiss his wife's hand as she arranged his pillows. All the morbid pride and distrust had left him forever. Full of this blessed confidence, this childlike humility, he slept.

The sound of bells awakened him. It came from the rude little Swedish church of the settlement.

" What are those bells ringing for?" he asked.

" They come from the church, I suppose,

dear Richard. It is Sunday, you know," answered Hannah, her eyes full of tears.

"Oh! Hannah," said Dick, "can you forgive me? I read Dennison's letter. I used to be jealous of him, and began to think they might influence you against me. When Mr. Lawrence at the planing-mill asked me to go down into the well he was having dug, I did not care what happened to me, and so I went, although I knew it was very dangerous. Can you forgive me, my own wife, for ever doubting your stanch devotion to me?"

Her arms were round his neck for reply, and their lips met in a kiss more fraught with deep feeling, more earnest with a love now sanctified by trial, then any they had ever known as lovers in long-past days at the old homestead.

* * * * * * * *

In the suburbs of Los Angeles, a pretty cottage with wide veranda stands in a garden full of flowers. Roses nod and blush and look in at the windows, and orange trees whose golden fruit and fragrant blossoms lend their own peculiar southern charms to the place are everywhere—in fact, the cottage stands in the midst of a grove of them.

At a neatly laid breakfast-table in a

small arbor sits a lady. By her side a lad of about six is restraining his appetite gallantly. His hands are decorously folded, but his eyes turn longingly toward the plate of white rolls, the fruit and honey with which the table is well supplied.

"Father will soon be here, Jack. I know you are hungry, but let us wait for him just a few minutes longer," the lady says, smiling kindly at the child. As she speaks the husband and father joins them.

Can this handsome, prosperous-looking, well-dressed man be Richard Barry? Dick, the ne'er-to-do-well, who was to drag Hannah down to poverty by his thriftless ways and love of drink? Surely, although his hair is white, his fine carriage and clear eyes, as well as the evidences of elegance and comfort about the cottage, all show this is not the home of a drunkard.

He has prospered greatly during his sojourn in California.

Frank Dennison married Ruth long ago, and Lawyer Keene wrote to Hannah offering her in behalf of his clients, Ruth and Mrs. McClean, a small yearly income from her portion of the estate in Illinois. But Dick and Hannah quietly refused to accept anything less than their rightful share.

And now this bright Sunday morning Dick, before taking his seat at the break- fast table, kisses his wife gently upon the forehead and lays beside her plate a bunch of fragrant violets, still wet with the dew.

" Why did you not come earlier, papa," asks Master Jack.

" My dear boy, it is Easter Sunday, and on that day, as long as I live and we are spared to each other, I shall always present mamma with a bunch of flowers. Shall I tell you why I do this, Jack? Well, it is in commemoration of an Easter morning long ago, when you were a baby, and your mother's love and courage, goodness and

wisdom brought me back from the grave
to the green fields and the glorious sun-
light, to your bright face, and dearer than
all, to a full knowledge of what it means
to have gained the priceless gift of a good
woman's love.   Look at your mother
well, Jack; she is little, but has such a
brave, big heart!   Oh, my lad, there are
few like her!"

"I know it," said Master Jack, nodding
gravely back to his father.